For Jasmine Coppard,
with love

Special thanks to
Mandy Archer

ORCHARD BOOKS
338 Euston Road, London NW1 3BH
Orchard Books Australia
Level 17/207 Kent Street, Sydney, NSW 2000
A Paperback Original

First published in 2012 by Orchard Books

A CIP catalogue record for this book is available
from the British Library.

ISBN 978 1 40831 597 2
1 3 5 7 9 10 8 6 4 2

Printed in Great Britain

The paper and board used in this paperback are natural recyclable
products made from wood grown in sustainable forests. The
manufacturing processes conform to the environmental regulations
of the country of origin.

Orchard Books is a division of Hachette Children's Books,
an Hachette UK company

www.hachette.co.uk

Keira
the Film Star
Fairy

by Daisy Meadows

ORCHARD

www.rainbowmagic.co.uk

Jack Frost's Spell

No more shall I lurk out of sight,
It's time I gave the world a fright!
Keira's magic things I'll steal,
To make a wicked movie reel.

If everything can't go my way,
Filmmakers shall rue the day!
A chill will fall on every scene,
Disaster for the silver screen.

The Silver Script

Contents

Setting
the Scene

"Look, there's Julianna Stewart!"
whispered Kirsty Tate. "Isn't her fairy
princess costume beautiful?"

Rachel Walker peeked round just as
Julianna walked past. The film star gave
the girls a friendly wink, then sat down
in a director's chair with her name on
the back to study her script.

"Who'd have thought a really famous actress like Julianna would come to Wetherbury village?" said Rachel.

"And who'd have thought that she'd be spending most of the school holidays in Mrs Croft's garden?" added Kirsty.

Mrs Croft was a friend of Kirsty's parents, a sweet old lady who had lived in Wetherbury for years. Her little thatched cottage with pretty, blossoming trees at the front often caught the eyes of tourists and passers-by. A few weeks ago when Mrs Croft had been working in her garden, an executive from a big film studio had pulled up outside. He wanted to book the cottage for a brand new film starring the famous actress Julianna Stewart. When Mrs Croft agreed, she became the talk of the village! Truckloads of set designers, lighting engineers and prop-makers had turned up to transform her garden into a magical world. Now filming on *The Starlight Chronicles* was about to begin.

"It was so kind of Mrs Croft to let us spend some time on set," said Rachel, watching the director talk through the next scene with his star.

Not only had Mrs Croft arranged for the friends to watch the rehearsals, but when she'd heard that Rachel was coming to stay with Kirsty for a week, the kind old lady had also managed to get the girls parts as extras!

The pair had been cast as magical fairies, handmaidens to Julianna's fairy princess in one of the most exciting scenes in the film. It was the perfect part for them both – Kirsty and Rachel knew lots about fairies! The two best friends had been secretly visiting Fairyland for some time. They never knew when one of the fairies would need their help, but they were always ready to protect their magical friends from mean Jack Frost and his naughty goblin servants.

"I can't wait to try on our costumes," said Kirsty. "I wonder if they'll be as beautiful as real fairy clothes?"

Rachel shook her head and smiled. All the sequins and glitter in the human world couldn't create a look as magical as seeing a real fairy fluttering in her finery! Before she could answer her friend, the director tapped his clipboard with a pen.

"Attention, everybody," he called. "I'd like to run this scene from the top. We start filming first thing tomorrow and there's still lots of work to do."

Kirsty and Rachel exchanged excited
looks as the set bustled with people.
Helpers known as runners fetched props
for the actors and showed the extras
where to stand. Sound and lighting
experts rigged up cables, while the
dancers practised their steps.
In this scene of
The Starlight
Chronicles
the fairy
princess
was
due to
greet the
prince
at a
sparkling
moonlit ball.

Kirsty and Rachel couldn't wait to hear the stars run through their lines! They watched as Julianna took her place in front of Chad Stenning, the actor cast as the fairy prince.

"And...action!" cried the director, giving a thumbs-up.

Julianna coughed shyly, then stepped forward.

"Your Highness," she said, bobbing in a dainty curtsey. "The air tingles with enchantment this evening. Shall we dance?"

Chad gave a deep bow. "Let the music wait a while. Please walk with me on the terrace. There is something I must say."

The crew watched spellbound as Chad offered his arm to Julianna and led her off the set.

"Excellent work!" announced the director, ticking a sheet on his clipboard. "Take five."

Rachel and Kirsty chatted while the cast took a quick break. Runners rushed round the director, fetching notes and passing messages to the crew.

"I haven't seen that runner before," whispered Rachel, nudging her friend's arm. "He seems in a terrible hurry."

Kirsty looked up as the runner elbowed his way past the actors, then snatched a script from the director's table. She tried to see his face, but it was hidden beneath a dark baseball cap. It was only when he knocked her chair on the way out of the garden that she spotted a glimpse of green skin.

"That's no runner," Kirsty said breathlessly. "It's a goblin!"

Right on Cue!

Rachel felt the back of her neck begin to tingle. If Jack Frost's goblins were in Wetherbury it could mean nothing but trouble! She followed Kirsty's gaze and saw that, sure enough, two warty green feet were poking out of the bottom of the stranger's trousers.

"That's a goblin all right," she said. "We'd better follow him!"

Kirsty nodded and jumped to her feet, just as the director called 'Action!' one more time. Before the girls could slip away, a group of actors rushed forward to act out a party scene in the enchanted garden.

"Good evening, Your Highness," piped up a girl in a fairy skirt.

The man next to her elbowed the girl in the ribs and hissed, "That's my line, silly!"

22

The director rolled his eyes. "Take it from the top, please."

"Attention, fairies! Sinner is derved," gabbled the man. "Oh no! I mean 'dinner is served'! Or does that line come later? I can't remember!"

"Let's move on," frowned the director, turning to Chad and Julianna.

The cast and crew waited for the leading man and lady to start speaking. But instead of repeating their lines, they were totally silent.

"Julianna?" called the director. "Julianna!"

Julianna looked helplessly at Chad.

"Is it m-me next?" she stuttered. "My mind's gone blank!"

The set fell into chaos as assistants scrabbled to track down the correct page in the script.

"I don't understand," whispered Rachel. "Chad and Julianna have been word perfect up to now. Something or *someone* is upsetting things."

"We must find that goblin!" Kirsty said.

Rachel pointed to a path made of stepping-stones that curved around the back of Mrs Croft's cottage. "He ran down there. Let's go!"

The girls hurried along the path, making their way into a pretty meadow behind the old cottage.

Normally the meadow was a quiet place dotted with wild flowers, but today it was packed full of mobile homes in all shapes and sizes. The actors and crew had arranged to stay here while *The Starlight Chronicles* was in production. Kirsty and Rachel zigzagged around refreshment tents, equipment cases and deckchairs, before the goblin's baseball cap disappeared behind a plush-looking silver trailer.

"That way!" cried Rachel, just as a rail of fancy fairy outfits trundled across the friends' path. A wardrobe mistress with a tape measure round her neck smiled apologetically, pushing the enormous rack of clothes.

"Coming through!" she cried. "Sorry, girls."

Kirsty sighed. "We'll never catch the goblin now. It'll be too late by the time we get past these costumes."

"Don't be downhearted," came a voice as pretty as a tinkly bell.

As the girls tried to step around the rail, a cascade of tiny scarlet stars began to shimmer above the last frock in the row. It was the beautiful rhinestone-encrusted evening dress that Julianna was due to wear in the final scene. The stars began to sparkle and fizz even more brightly until – *pop!* – a pretty fairy burst out of the dress, landing on the rail near to Kirsty and Rachel.

"Hi!" she smiled. "I'm Keira the Film Star Fairy. You're just the friends I hoped to see today."

"Hello!" replied Kirsty and Rachel, their cheeks flushing with excitement.

The fairy fluttered her tiny gossamer wings, beckoning for the girls to follow her. As they dashed behind the next trailer, Keira's long scarlet gown swished in the breeze. It was stitched in the finest fairy satin, decorated with glittering rhinestones. A gold starburst slide glistened in Keira's dark hair.

"It's my job to look after movie-makers in Fairyland and the human world," she explained, when she was certain that no one else was nearby. "I've been watching over Julianna's career for a long time. She always shows such kindness to the animals she meets on location, and the fairies would like to say thank you. I'm here to help make *The Starlight Chronicles* a hit!"

Kirsty and Rachel listened carefully as Keira went on to explain that she'd brought three magical objects with her.

"The silver script makes sure that actors get their lines right every time. The magical megaphone helps directors organise everyone on set and the enchanted clapperboard gets the cameras rolling. Everything was going beautifully," she sighed, "until Jack Frost decided to have a go at being a film star, too."

The troubled fairy told the girls how the Ice Lord had sent his goblins out to Wetherbury. Their instructions were to snatch the silver script and bring it back to Jack Frost's Ice Castle!

"Julianna and the other actors won't be able to perform properly without the script," said Keira, looking worried. "Will you please help me get it back?"

Goblin Glade

"Of course we'll help!" cried Rachel. "We'd do anything for the fairies."

"We just saw one of Jack Frost's goblins steal a script from the director's table," revealed Kirsty. "He ran behind that shiny trailer up ahead."

"That must be my silver script!" gasped Keira. "I bet he's trying to take it back to the Ice Castle. Who knows what mischief he'll cause with it?"

"If we run past those caravans I'm sure we can catch him up," said Rachel, leading the way.

Kirsty opened the top pocket of her jacket so that Keira could flutter inside.

"No one will see you in here," she said.

Keira peeped over the edge of Kirsty's pocket as the friends picked their way across the grassy meadow.

When they got to the gate at the other side, the goblin had disappeared.

The friends and Keira found themselves on the edge of a winding lane that led out of the village.

"I'll find out where the goblins have gone," said Keira, and waved her wand in the air. A haze of gold stars began to shimmer at its tip. The little fairy then moved her wand around to point in different directions. The stars got much brighter when it was pointing at the woods.

"This way!" cried the fairy.

Kirsty and Rachel ran to the edge of the wood, then peeped through the trees.

"I can see the goblin," gasped Rachel, pointing to a shady glade filled with ferns. "And he's not alone!"

There, in the dappled afternoon light, the goblin was pacing up and down with the silver script in his hand. His cap had been thrown down, revealing his hooked nose. He was holding his chin up as if making a grand speech. Behind him, a short goblin and a goblin with very big ears were muttering together and shaking their heads.

"What's going on?" wondered Kirsty. "When Jack Frost sends his servants out to steal something, he usually wants to get his hands on it straight away."

"I think the goblins have decided to have a bit of fun first," said Keira. "The one with the script is reading out lines from it!"

"How funny! Who'd have thought that goblins would like play-acting?" chuckled Rachel.

The girls crept slowly closer and crouched behind a blackberry bush so they could listen in.

"*I* have to be the director!" shouted
the hook-nosed goblin. "It was me who
found the silver script, and if you won't
do as I say I'll tell Jack Frost what you're
up to!"

"Only if I can be the
prince," snapped the
big-eared goblin.

The short goblin
kicked the tree next
to him so hard
the bump echoed
round the glade.
"That means I have
to play the princess," he
grumbled. "Yuk!"

The 'director' sniggered, and then
pushed the goblin 'prince' down onto
one knee.

"Action!" he grunted, clapping his hands together. As they shut, his fingers knocked the prince's pointy nose.

"Ouch!" snapped the prince. "Will thou marry me, sweet princess?"

Keira fluttered silently out of Kirsty's pocket, coming to rest on a branch.

"Oh my!" she gasped. "They're acting out the proposal scene from *The Starlight Chronicles*. This is where Chad's character asks Julianna to become his fairy bride. It's supposed to be romantic."

"Go on then," yelled the hook-nosed director goblin, pointing at the ugly princess. "Pucker up for a kiss."

"Not on your nelly!" thundered the goblin princess.

The goblin prince snatched the script out of the director's hands, and hit the princess over the head.

Within moments, the goblins' secret read-through had turned into pandemonium. The green trio tugged and pulled at the script, shaking their fists at each other, making threats and calling out nasty names.

The girls and Keira ducked back behind the blackberry bush, trying hard not to giggle out loud.

"This little performance has given me an idea," whispered Rachel. "If it works, we should be able to trick the goblins into handing the silver script over to us."

"What shall we do?" asked Keira, her eyes shining with excitement.

As Rachel leant in to share her plan with Keira and Kirsty, a twig caught on her jumper. It snapped with a loud *crack!*

"Who's there?" bellowed the goblin director, peering through the trees.

"Oh no!" gasped Kirsty. "We've been caught!"

Putting on an Act

Rachel's heart began to thump. They were going to have to put her plan into action more quickly than she had thought!

"All we've got to do is pretend that we know lots about making films," she whispered. "Keira, would you be able to cast a spell to give us some smart clothes? We need to disguise ourselves as Hollywood talent-spotters."

"Of course!" replied Keira, sprinkling a handful of fairy dust onto the friends. A fountain of golden sparkles shimmered over Kirsty and Rachel, transforming their outfits into grown-up business suits. They each felt a pair of dark sunglasses slip over their eyes.

"Now we look like real movie scouts," exclaimed Rachel. "Thank you, Keira!"

Kirsty carefully opened her top pocket so that the fairy could hide again.

"Good thinking," said Keira. "If the
goblins spot me, they'll realise that we've
come for the silver script."

When Keira was safely hidden, Kirsty
and Rachel leapt up from behind the
blackberry bush.

"Yoo-hoo!
Over here!"
they cried,
waving their
arms in the
air to get
the goblins'
attention.

The
goblin
director peered through the glade. When
he saw the two girls, his face broke into a
horrible scowl.

"What are you looking at?" snapped the goblin who was playing the prince. Rachel stepped into the clearing.

"We were walking through this wood scouting movie locations," she announced, putting on an American accent. "We heard your performance and thought you might like a few tips. Your fairy princess looks very pretty, but your fairy prince is completely unbelievable!"

"Hah!" the goblin princess jeered at the prince.

"And what about you?" piped up Kirsty, pointing to the goblin director. "Surely you can get the actors to do better than that? I've never heard such feeble direction!"

The director snatched the silver script back off the big-eared goblin prince, clutching it closely to his chest.

"What do you know about films?" he sniffed. "Seen a few on TV?"

The goblins liked that joke. The director stuck his tongue out and waggled his fingers, while the other two blew noisy raspberries.

47

Rachel waited quietly until the gang
had finished.

"We're working on the movie that's
being filmed in the village," she replied.
"If you listen to our advice, I'm sure
you three could put on a polished
performance too."

The hook-nosed goblin director pouted
and shrugged his shoulders.

"I suppose we
could do with
a little help,"
he admitted,
"to uncover
our star
potential."

Rachel
tried to hide
her smile.

"Let's start with a few acting exercises," she nodded. "I'll give you a scene to imagine, then you three have to act out what the characters might say. It's called improvising."

The goblin who had been playing the part of the fairy prince scratched his head.

"That sounds way too difficult," he sulked.

"Not if you think about it," encouraged Rachel. "Just try."

Kirsty held her breath. Goblins didn't like thinking too much.

"What about me?" complained the goblin director. "If the other two try this improvising thing, how am I supposed to boss them about?"

"You don't need a director when you're improvising," replied Rachel. "You're *all* going to have a go at acting."

The goblin director glared at the goblin actors. Ordering them around had been the best thing about this film lark!

"So," asked Rachel. "Are you going to do it or not?"

A Perfect Performance

The goblin director paced up and down the glade, still clutching the silver script.

"Come on!" yelled the goblin who had been playing the fairy princess. "If I've had to read a stinky girl part, you should take a turn at acting too."

The hook-nosed goblin director screwed up his face.

"Shan't!" he squawked, turning his back on the girls.

"That's a shame," sighed Rachel. "I was going to give you the starring role."

That decided it. The goblin was far too vain to give up a star part!

"I'll do it!" he cried, elbowing his two cronies out of the way.

"Imagine that you're a great writer who's just finished a really amazing new book," said Rachel. "Kirsty is going to play your publisher."

"Pretend you're coming to my office to deliver the story," Kirsty said.

The vain goblin puffed out his chest.

"That's easy!" he declared. "Just leave it to me."

The other two goblins scowled as if they were both about to complain. They didn't want to miss out on the limelight!

Rachel thought quickly.

"You two will play the writer's children," she decided. "Stay in the background for the moment."

55

"That's not fair!" shouted both goblins at the same time.

"Don't worry," said Rachel. "Your big scene comes next."

"Are we ready to start?" asked Kirsty. "Then... action!"

The hook-nosed goblin swaggered across the glade, holding the silver script up in the air.

"I'm here to see my publisher!" he announced, pretending to knock on an imaginary door. "My masterpiece is ready!"

The goblin tried to make his voice sound very grand and clever. Watching through the trees, the other goblins forgot their parts and started to snigger.

"Please come in," replied Kirsty, playing along with the scene.

"I think you'll enjoy reading this," continued the goblin, handing her the silver script. "It's very special."

At that instant, Keira burst out of Kirsty's pocket. Quickly, the fairy swished through the air, a trail of golden stars fizzing behind her.

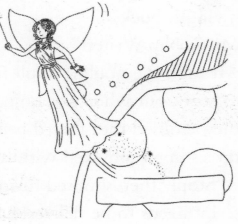

She tapped the silver script lightly with her wand, magically shrinking it down to fairy-size.

"It *is* special!" Keira laughed. "Thank you for giving it back, Mr Goblin Writer!"

It took the goblins a full five seconds to work out what was going on. When they realised that they'd been tricked, the threesome squawked with rage.

"Stop!" they shouted furiously. "That script needs to be delivered to Jack Frost!"

The goblins lunged and jumped for the enchanted papers, but Keira did a swift loop-the-loop high in the air above them.

"This is going back to Fairyland," she told them. "Where it belongs."

"What are we going to do now?" snapped the hook-nosed goblin. "I'm not telling Jack Frost."

"Me neither!" howled the goblin with the big ears.

The hook-nosed
goblin was
scrambling
into the
woods.
"Time
to hide!"
he wailed.

When the silly threesome had finally
disappeared, Keira smiled at Kirsty
and Rachel.

"Thank you so much," she exclaimed,
magically changing the girls back
into their normal clothes. "Now actors
everywhere will be able to play their
parts properly. See you again soon!"

The Film Star Fairy tucked the silver
script under her arm, vanishing in a
shimmer of fairy dust.

"Goodbye!" Rachel called after her. "It was lovely to meet you."

Kirsty pointed the way towards Mrs Croft's cottage.

"Let's go back to the film set," she suggested. "I'll bet those rehearsals are on track again!"

"I hope so," Rachel replied, "but we should keep an extra special eye out for those goblins. Who knows what Jack Frost will do when he can't get his hands on the silver script? He won't give up that easily."

Kirsty nodded, linking arms with Rachel. Whatever happened, the girls would be there to help their fairy friends!

The Magical Megaphone

Contents

A Cast in Chaos

"We're here just in time!" said Rachel, opening Mrs Croft's back gate. "Now that Keira's got the silver script, the rehearsals can start again."

The girls could already hear the director's voice across the garden. He was reading out a list of names through his megaphone. All the actors playing fairies and elves were asked to gather under the blossom trees.

"Everybody is to be in costume please," called the director. "The engagement party scene is going to be a full dress rehearsal."

"Let's hurry," exclaimed Kirsty. "I don't want to miss a thing!"

The friends scurried back along the stepping-stones that skirted around Mrs Croft's cottage. Actors dressed as elves rushed past them, buttoning up velvet jackets. The wardrobe mistress the girls had met earlier was busy helping fairy cast members slip on gauzy wings dotted with sequins. A props lady was handing out sparkly wands.

"Let's sit over there," suggested Rachel, pointing to a wooden bench tucked away beside the garden pond.

Kirsty happily took her seat, admiring the fountain that bubbled in the middle of the pond, rainbow colours dancing in its spray. This was the perfect place to watch a magical fairy rehearsal!

"There's Julianna!" Kirsty whispered, pointing across the garden.

The film's leading lady stepped out from underneath a pink blossom tree. Julianna had a towelling robe over her costume and a silk scarf tied loosely around her hair. She was listening closely to the director's instructions for the next scene. Chad was standing by some roses, waiting for a make-up lady to powder his nose.

"At least we know Julianna and Chad won't forget their lines now," murmured Rachel, relieved that the silver script was out of goblin hands.

"We'll start filming under the
trees," called the director through his
megaphone, "then the fairy servants
should follow the princess as she flutters
on to the rose arch."

Kirsty and Rachel both watched in
admiration. Julianna had slipped her robe
off her shoulders,
revealing her
lovely lilac
gown.
The star
untied her
headscarf
and handed it
to her assistant.
A diamond tiara
twinkled on top of her hair, which had
been curled in pretty golden ringlets.

"She really does look like a fairy princess!" whispered Rachel.

"Let's roll!" announced the director.

The cast and crew fell silent, waiting for Julianna to say her first line. Instead, the actress delicately lifted the hem of her skirt and walked towards the rose arch.

"The royal celebrations are ready to begin!" she cried, curtseying in front of Chad. "All of my ladies-in-waiting should be in attendance."

Chad looked very confused – he was still having his make-up done!

The director picked up his megaphone.

"Miss Stewart," he said gently. "You're too early! The lines with your fairy servants should take place under the blossom tree. *Then* you move across to greet the prince at the rose arch."

"That's not what you said," she muttered, wrinkling her nose.

The director coughed politely and shook his head.

"Can we try again?" he called. "Everyone go back to the blossom tree."

Julianna took her place back under the tree, and then began to recite her lines. But when she turned to speak to her co-stars, her fairy servants had vanished from sight.

"Ladies-in-waiting!" bellowed the director. "Where are you?"

Three actresses wearing peach chiffon dresses peeped out from under the rose arch.

"We're over here," replied one. "Just where you told us!"

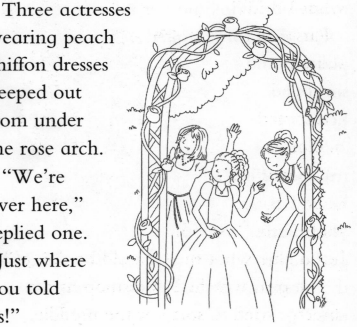

"And now there's no room for me!" complained Chad, marching towards the trees. "I'm going to stand with Julianna."

The frustrated director shook his megaphone in the air.

"No, no, no!" he wailed. "That's not what I said!"

Kirsty and Rachel swapped concerned glances.

"Something's gone wrong," said Kirsty. "No one has a clue what they should be doing!"

The girls watched in dismay as the director tried to sort out the muddle.

Every instruction he shouted through the megaphone seemed to make things worse. After a few more minutes even *he* seemed to have forgotten where he wanted his actors to stand!

The rehearsal was in chaos. Confused actors stormed back to their trailers, leaving the crew to argue over what to do next.

"This is awful!" declared Rachel. "What shall we do?"

Suddenly the fountain in front of the friends began to bubble higher, shooting up a spray of silvery water. There, rising on the crest of the cascade, was Keira! The fairy waved at Kirsty and Rachel, but her little face looked pale with worry.

Keira beckoned the girls over to the bushes at the back of the garden.

"Will you come with me to Fairyland?" she gasped. "We haven't got much time!"

Seeing Pool Surprise

Keira explained that Queen Titania had made a special request for Kirsty and Rachel's help.

"Her Majesty will tell you everything when we get to Fairyland," urged the Film Star Fairy. "If you'll come?"

"Of course!" cried both girls at once.

A whirl of fairy magic
spun around
the friends,
surrounding
them in a
flurry of
golden stars.
Kirsty and
Rachel felt
themselves
suddenly

getting smaller and smaller until they
were transformed into fairies, with
shimmering wings on their shoulders.

The friends joined hands, then flew
towards the fountain. Sunbeams danced
in the spray, dazzling the threesome with
their rainbow lights. Kirsty and Rachel
closed their eyes.

When they opened them again, they were gliding above the emerald hills of Fairyland! The hills were dotted with the scarlet rooftops of toadstool houses, and every so often a fairy opened a window to wave hello.

Before they knew it, the glittering pink towers of the Fairyland Palace came into view. The friends landed gently in front of a pair of hedges that were trimmed in the shape of peacocks.

Keira led the way through the hedges into a lovely walled garden. Little paths meandered up and down the lawns, lined with pretty shells and colourful flowers. In the middle there was a pond filled with exquisite water lilies. Kirsty and Rachel recognised this as the magical Seeing Pool. Queen Titania was standing next to the pool, her arm held out in welcome. The girls rushed over and curtsied.

"Hello again, dear girls!" the queen said warmly.

"Your Majesty," said Rachel breathlessly. "We came as soon as we could."

"We're here to help in any way we can," added Kirsty.

The queen smiled at the girls, but her eyes looked troubled.

"Thank you," she said with a gracious nod. "I asked Keira to fetch you both because *The Starlight Chronicles* is in serious trouble."

83

Rachel and Kirsty swapped worried glances.

"What has happened?" asked Rachel.

Queen Titania stepped towards the Seeing Pool and waved her magic wand. The trickling waters instantly stilled and cleared.

"Come closer," she said, as the pool began to shine with magical light.

Kirsty, Rachel and Keira gazed into the enchanted waters.

A picture of Jack
Frost slowly
formed on the
surface. The
Ice Lord's face
was creased
into an angry
scowl.

"That's Mrs Croft's
garden!" gasped Rachel, noticing the
blossom trees behind him. "What's he
doing there?"

"When his goblins didn't bring back
the silver script, Jack Frost got tired of
waiting for them," explained Keira. "He
stormed all the way to Wetherbury to
find out what was going on!"

"He really has got his heart set on
becoming a film star," said Kirsty.

When the friends looked into the
Seeing Pool again, it showed the meanie
snooping around the film set. Kirsty
and Rachel frowned as he picked up a
megaphone hanging on
the back of the
director's chair.
He peered left
and right to
check that
the coast was
clear, then
stuffed the
megaphone
underneath his
spiky purple cloak,
cackling in delight. The friends shuddered
as they heard him boast about taking the
loot back to his frosty home.

"He shouldn't take things that don't belong to him," said Kirsty, as the picture faded into bubbles. "The director needs that megaphone to do his job!"

"It's not just *any* megaphone," added Keira. "Jack Frost snatched my magical megaphone. I'd loaned it to *The Starlight Chronicles* to make sure filming went well! But if it's locked away in his Ice Castle, the director will find it impossible to get everyone organised."

Rachel thought back to the disastrous rehearsal. No wonder everything had been going wrong! How were they going to get the magical megaphone back?

An Ear-splitting Scene

"Would you be willing to go with Keira to Jack Frost's Ice Castle?" Queen Titania asked the girls. "The magical megaphone must be found and returned."

Kirsty and Rachel both nodded their heads.

"Of course, Your Majesty," said Kirsty.

"Thank you, dear friends," said the queen, lifting up her wand once again. "The magical megaphone should be easy to find. Its sound can travel for miles."

Queen Titania pointed her wand up to the sky. A shimmer of multi-coloured fairy dust sparkled and flashed all around the fairies.

When the fairy dust finally settled, the beautiful palace gardens had disappeared. Instead Kirsty, Rachel and Keira found themselves in a dark wood.

A biting wind blew through the icy trees, making the fairies shiver. "We're in Jack Frost's kingdom now," whispered Keira. "The Ice Castle is just on the other side of this wood."

Suddenly a chilling voice echoed round the trees.

"You goblins are useless!" it cried.

"That sounds like Jack Frost!" gasped Rachel, looking nervously around her. Where is he?"

The fairies fluttered up into the dark branches to listen again. The sinister voice ranted and raved, carried on the freezing wind.

"All you had to do was bring back the silver script!" it bellowed. "I should have swiped it myself!"

Kirsty looked left and right, but the Ice Lord was nowhere to be seen.

"He must be shouting through the magical megaphone!" guessed Keira. "Let's follow the noise."

Keira darted into the dark clouds
swirling above the forest. Up there, the
fairies could see jagged snow-capped
mountains and the frosty-blue turrets
of the Ice Castle jutting out from the
surrounding gloom.

Rachel, Kirsty and Keira flew straight
towards the castle. As they got closer,
Jack Frost's angry shouts boomed louder
and louder.

"Watch out for the goblin guards!"
said Rachel, as the friends landed on the
castle battlements.

Kirsty looked along the ramparts. At one end, she could see a pair of goblins on sentry duty, but they weren't paying attention at all. They were wobbling backwards and  forwards, their palms pressed to their ears. The fairies slipped past them, fluttering down to the castle courtyard.

Down on the ground, the noise was almost unbearable. Kirsty ducked behind a pillar, then peeped back out.

Keira fluttered forward, but darted
back the instant she spotted
Jack Frost. The Ice
Lord was pacing
around the
courtyard,
giving his
goblins
a terrible
telling-off.

"There are
the goblins
who stole
the silver
script," Keira
murmured to her
friends. "Jack Frost's
shouting at them through the magical
megaphone!"

The poor henchmen were in a very sorry state. As well as the naughty ones who had tried to steal the silver script, a mob of other goblins had been summoned from all over the castle. Some had their fingers in their ears, others had flannels pressed against their foreheads. Jack Frost's noisy shouting was giving the goblins dreadful headaches, but he didn't care a bit.

"Listen to me!" thundered Jack Frost at the top of his voice. "You lot need to start work on my first film! I want you to snatch some cameras and spotlights. I'm going to need a director's chair too…"

"We have to stop him," urged Kirsty, forced to shout over the din.

Rachel held her hands up to her head.

"But we can't get any closer," she cried. "The noise is deafening!"

Silence is Golden

Kirsty and Rachel watched as the goblins tried to make sense of Jack Frost's ear-splitting demands. With their fingers in their ears, the servants were getting in a terrible muddle. There were goblins bumping into each other, some tripping over and others wailing in protest at the horrible noise.

"We must do something!" urged Kirsty. "Jack Frost is sure to get up to mischief now he's got the magical megaphone!"

"What was that?" called Rachel, as the shouts got even louder. "I can't hear you!"

Kirsty frowned. It was impossible to hear a tiny fairy voice over this racket! Luckily, Keira knew just what to do.

She lightly tapped her wand against her ear, then whispered a spell to stop the horrible din:

"*Fairy magic, all around,*
Find a way to stop this sound!"

There was a flurry of golden stars as each of the friends suddenly felt a pair of earplugs slip into their ears.

Kirsty gave Keira a thumbs-up, enjoying the quiet. Even though they still couldn't hear each other, it was lovely to shut out Jack Frost's booming orders. She couldn't help thinking that the goblins would feel much better if they had earplugs too...

'That's it!' thought Kirsty. Keira had just given her a wonderful idea!

Keira watched Kirsty point to the earplugs in her own ears and then wave over to the goblins. The clever little fairy understood at once. If the goblins had earplugs too, they wouldn't be able to hear any of Jack Frost's scheming plans!

Keira gently tapped her ear with her wand once again, repeating the spell at the top of her voice. The wand sent a burst of golden stars streaming into the courtyard. The glittering stars whisked over Jack Frost's head, but he was too busy ranting to look up. One by one, the stars landed on the goblins stumbling around the yard. As they touched the clueless servants, a pair of earplugs slid into their ears. Soon every goblin in the castle was wearing them.

"Peace at last," grinned one.

"Can't hear a word now," boomed his crony. "Brilliant!"

Jack Frost chose that moment to hand out a job to each of the goblins. He pointed a bony finger at each one in turn. The goblins stared gormlessly, not making sense of a word.

"Step to it, then!" he thundered, once he'd finished. "You've all got lots to do!"

The goblins didn't budge an inch. Instead of moving, they carried on gawping at their master. Jack Frost screwed his face into an angry scowl.

"*Step to it!*" he repeated, bellowing even louder into the magical megaphone. "You heard me! Get on with it!"

Keira, Kirsty and Rachel shared a silent smile. They couldn't hear what Jack Frost was saying, but they could tell their plan was starting to work!

The goblins began to mill aimlessly around the courtyard. Without clear orders they were useless! They could see that Jack Frost was trying to say something, but not one of them fancied taking their earplugs out again.

The Ice Lord's face was turning purple with rage.

"What's wrong with this thing?" he snarled, shaking the megaphone and peering inside it.

Rachel spotted her chance. As quick as a flash, she darted inside the other end of the magical megaphone.

Jack Frost narrowed his eyes, trying to see what was suddenly blocking his view. Rachel wriggled up through the megaphone and burst out of the other end, right into Jack Frost's face!

"Arrghh!" yelled the meanie, jumping back in shock.

Keira zoomed out from behind the pillar, rushing eagerly towards her precious possession.

"That's mine!" she cried happily, lifting the magical megaphone high into the air. As soon as her little hand touched it it shrank down to fairy-size.

Jack Frost howled in anger.

"Goblins!" he ordered. "Grab those fairies, now!"

Back to Fairyland

Kirsty and Rachel followed Keira up into the air, taking care to flutter out of Jack Frost's reach.

"Pesky fairies!" he fumed. "Come back here or I'll set my goblins on you!"

The meanie glared at his servants, but they simply grunted, shrugged and scratched their heads.

"They can't hear a word that he's saying!" chuckled Keira, pulling her earplugs out. The Film Star Fairy beckoned for Kirsty and Rachel to do the same, then all three sets of plugs magically disappeared into thin air.

The goblins could have thrown their earplugs on the ground too, but they weren't clever enough to think of that.

"What a gormless bunch!" barked Jack Frost, storming up and down the courtyard. "Can't you lot do *anything* I tell you?"

"What's up
with him?"
sniffed one of
the goblins,
nudging a pal
in the ribs.
The other goblin
gawped at his master
then pulled a silly face.
"Lucky we've got these
earplugs in!" he sniggered.

"Time to go!" beamed Keira, pointing
her wand at Kirsty and Rachel. The
happy little fairy's cheeks glowed with
pleasure as a dazzling fizz of stars
whisked the trio far away from the Ice
Castle. The last thing that Kirsty and
Rachel could hear was Jack Frost's
shouts echoing in the distance.

"That was quick!" gasped Rachel, soon spotting the familiar pink towers of the Fairyland Palace shining up ahead.

"Look!" added Kirsty. "There's Queen Titania."

The friends landed gracefully in the palace garden, just beside the enchanted Seeing Pool.

"Welcome back!" said the queen, walking over to greet them.

Keira's eyes danced with pleasure as she held up the magical object for the queen to see.

"The magical megaphone is safe," the fairy said with a smile. "Thanks to Kirsty and Rachel."

Queen Titania held out her hands to the girls.

"I cannot thank you enough for your help," she said. "Now directors everywhere will be able to carry on making films for us all to enjoy."

Kirsty and Rachel both bobbed a curtsey, then turned round to share a hug with Keira.

Helping the Film Star Fairy again had been an amazing adventure, but it was time that they went back to Mrs Croft's garden. The best friends felt much happier knowing that the dress rehearsal could now run without a hitch.

"Goodbye, Keira," said Rachel. "We'll let you know how the filming goes on *The Starlight Chronicles*."

"Yes, please!" replied Keira. "Now that the magical megaphone is safe, I'm sure that Julianna will put in a sparkling performance."

Kirsty told Keira and the queen about an extra-special scene that they were filming the next day. She and Rachel were due to play their parts as extras in the grand fairy wedding!

"Would you like to come and watch, Keira?" asked Rachel.

Keira's face flushed with pleasure.

"Thank you, girls!" she replied. "That's definitely a date!"

After everyone had said goodbye, Keira hugged Kirsty and Rachel. With a wave of her wand, she turned them back to human-size and sent them whizzing back home. The next time the friends met, the girls would be in front of the cameras!

"This holiday is going to be hard to beat," laughed Kirsty as they arrived in Mrs Croft's garden.

"It's about to get even more exciting," added Rachel, "Tomorrow we're going to be film stars!"

The Enchanted Clapperboard

Contents

Camera Catastrophe

"Take your places, everyone!" called the director. "We're filming in five minutes."

Kirsty and Rachel were both feeling very excited. It was finally time for them to play their parts as extras in *The Starlight Chronicles*.

"I can't wait to show our costumes
to Keira," whispered Kirsty, smoothing
down her frothy
net skirt.

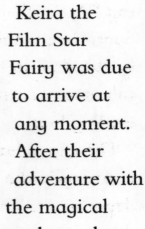

Keira the
Film Star
Fairy was due
to arrive at
any moment.
After their
adventure with
the magical
megaphone the
day before, she had promised to come
and watch them filming their scene.

"You look just like a fairy handmaiden,"
said Rachel, giving Kirsty a happy smile.

"You too," replied her best friend.

The girls had butterflies in their

tummies, but
they couldn't
wait to hear
the director
say "Action!"
Soon they would
be standing in front of the camera with
Julianna Stewart, the film's beautiful
leading lady.

The extras had spent a wonderful
morning in the hair and make-up
department. The wardrobe lady had
dressed each girl in a pale-pink gown,
made of floaty material and embroidered
with tiny sparkling stones. Their hair was
curled into tumbling ringlets and topped
with twinkling tiaras. Filmy chiffon
wings completed their transformation
into fairy handmaidens.

The first scene to be filmed was in the fairy princess's bedroom. The pretty set had been built inside Mrs Croft's quaint old cottage. Kirsty, Rachel and the other extras would be attending the fairy princess on the morning of her wedding.

"I hope I can remember where to stand!" said an extra called Angel.

Her friend, Emily, bent down to tie the ribbons on her satin slippers.

"Oh, my hands are trembling with excitement!" she said breathlessly.

"Just do what I do," said a sweet voice. "You're all going to be wonderful, I know it!"

Rachel and Kirsty spun around to see Julianna stepping onto the film set. The star looked radiant in her flowing gown. The skirts swished as she moved, making each shimmering layer catch the light beautifully. She was carrying a bridal bouquet of peach blossom from Mrs Croft's garden.

"You look perfect!" exclaimed Rachel, remembering the real fairy princess bride they'd met with Kate the Royal Wedding Fairy.

Julianna smiled happily at the girls.

"Thank you," she replied. "Break a leg, everyone!" Angel and Emily looked confused. "That's how actors say 'good luck'," explained Julianna. "It's an old theatre tradition."

The film crew came into the room and started to get the cameras ready.

Large, dazzling spotlights shone onto
the sparkling set as the director held
up his special movie clapperboard.
Kirsty and Rachel held their breath
with excitement.

"Here we go," the director said.
"Quiet on set, please. Lights, camera..."

The girls waited to hear the word 'action', but nothing happened.

"The clapperboard is stuck," said the director, frowning.

The flustered crew tried to get the clapperboard working again, but it refused to snap shut. An  assistant ran up and passed the director two thick wooden sticks.

"I found these in the props department," he explained.

The director grabbed the sticks, and then called for everyone to be quiet.

"Lights, camera... ACTION!"

Kirsty, Rachel and the other extras began to arrange the fairy princess's dress, just as they had been told. The girls tried very hard not to look into the cameras that surrounded them.

"This is my last daybreak as a fairy princess," said Julianna. "Today I shall become a—"

"Stop, please!" cried a voice, cutting Julianna's speech short.

"Who said that?" demanded the director.

One of the camera operators waved his hand to get the director's attention.

"My camera just…stopped," he stammered. "I can't understand it."

The director frowned, then held up the pieces of wood and clapped them together again.

"One more time, please," he called. "From the top."

"That means 'from the start'," Julianna whispered to the girls.

She started to say her lines, but then there was a loud cry from the back of the room.

"My camera won't record!" exclaimed a second camera operator.

Another operator scratched her head. "Mine's the same!"

The exasperated director jumped down from his chair. Everyone on the set gathered around the cameras and started talking at once.

"Something funny is going on around here," whispered Rachel. "I can feel it!"

Keira's News

The director stomped out of the room in search of more cameras, and the rest of the film crew trailed after him, chattering loudly. The other extras followed them, but Kirsty grabbed Rachel's arm.

"Wait," she said quietly. "Look – that camera's glowing!"

The friends stared as the shimmer
spread around the camera lens. Then, in
a flurry of golden stars, Keira whooshed
out of the lens. The
tiny fairy darted
into the room
and hovered
in front of
the girls.

"I'm so glad
you're here!"
said Rachel
in excitement.

But Keira didn't look happy at all.

"Oh girls, something terrible's
happened," she said. "While I was
getting ready to come here, Jack Frost
broke into my film studio and stole my
enchanted clapperboard!"

Rachel and
Kirsty were
horrified.
"He
was very
angry
when we
took the
magical
megaphone
back again,"
remembered Kirsty.
"I bet this is his revenge!"

"What does the enchanted clapperboard
do?" asked Rachel.

"It makes sure that filming always goes
to plan," Keira explained. "Without it,
even a big budget blockbuster will end
in disaster."

"That must be why filming is going wrong today," guessed Kirsty. "We haven't even been able to film one scene. Where could Jack Frost have hidden it?"

Keira looked even more worried than she had before.

"All we know is that he gave the enchanted clapperboard to his goblins," she said.

Suddenly there was a muffled, squawking giggle from outside the door, followed by the sound of footsteps on the stairs. The friends looked at each other in surprise.

"That sounded like a goblin," said
Kirsty. "Do you think one of them
could have brought the enchanted
clapperboard *here*?"

"He was going upstairs," Rachel
added. "Oh no! There's another crew
filming in Mrs Croft's guest bedroom."

"We can't let him disturb any more
filming," said Keira. "Come on!"

The Film Star
Fairy darted
under Rachel's
ringlets, and
then the girls
ran out of
the room
and up the
old wooden
staircase.

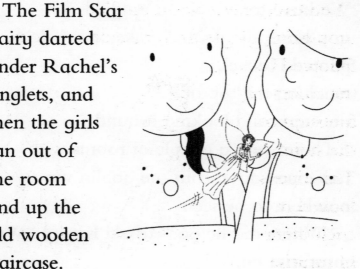

They were just
in time to
see a green
goblin foot
disappearing
around the
top of the
landing.

"A goblin!
We have to
stop him,"
panted Rachel,
reaching the top of
the stairs and looking around.

There were a couple of rooms with
half-open doors, but the goblin was
nowhere to be seen.

"Where did he go?" asked Kirsty. "We
must find him!"

"We can't just walk into the rooms," said Rachel. "If the film crew see us, they'll send us downstairs."

"Let me turn you into fairies," said Keira. "That will make it easier to search around without being seen."

"Good idea!" said Rachel.

Keira waved her wand and a cascade of golden fairy dust fizzed from its tip, sprinkling over the girls' heads. It twinkled in their hair and they shrank to fairy-size in the blink of an eye.

Soon they were no taller than Mrs
Croft's skirting board. They fluttered the
filmy wings that
had appeared
on their
shoulders.

Rachel
whizzed
into the air
and looped
the loop
– it was
wonderful
to be a fairy again!

Suddenly they heard a muffled squeak
from behind the nearest door, which was
slightly ajar.

"I'd recognise that sound anywhere,"
said Kirsty. "Goblins! Come on!"

One by one, the three friends swooped through the crack in the door into Mrs Croft's bedroom. Sure enough, two goblins were bouncing up and down on the bed as if it were a trampoline. One was plump, and the other was skinny with a warty nose.

Rachel clutched Kirsty's arm in excitement. The goblin with the warty nose had a large clapperboard under his arm!

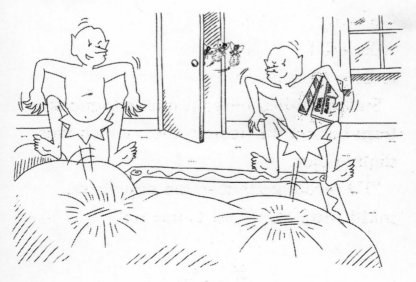

Goblin Hide and Seek

"That's the enchanted clapperboard!" said Keira. "Oh, those naughty goblins!"

"It's my turn to play with it," the plump goblin was complaining in a loud whine. "You've had it for ages. Jack Frost told us to bring it here and learn about making films, and that's what I want to do!"

The skinny
goblin turned
a somersault
and held
on to the
enchanted
clapperboard
even more
tightly.
"Why should
you have it?" he
squawked. "It's mine!"

"It doesn't belong to either of you!"
declared Rachel, fluttering forward.
"Give it back to Keira right now!"

"Fairies!" cried the skinny goblin.

He lost his balance and bounced off the
bed with a loud crash.

"Shhh!" said the three friends together.

They didn't want the film crew to come in and find the goblins! The skinny goblin stood up, rubbing his head and scowling.

"That was your fault," he said. "Silly, pesky fairies!"

"Give me back my enchanted clapperboard!" Keira demanded.

"Shan't!" snapped the goblin.

He raced to the door, wrenched it open and shot out at top speed. The plump goblin followed him, and Kirsty groaned.

"We have to stop them before the film crew sees them," she said.

"And we have to get the enchanted clapperboard back," Rachel added. "Otherwise the whole film will be completely ruined!"

Keira, Rachel and Kirsty zoomed out onto the landing. At the top of the stairs, the goblins were playing tug-of-war with the enchanted clapperboard.

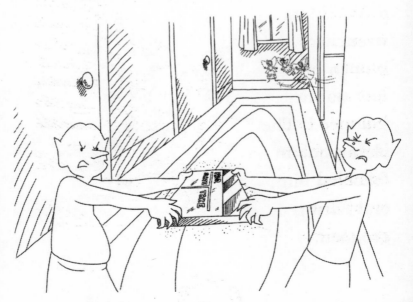

"Mine!" squawked the plump goblin, yanking the magical object towards him.

"Mine!" wailed the warty goblin, pulling just as hard.

Suddenly, the girls heard footsteps coming from behind one of the closed doors.

"What was that noise?" said a voice.

"Someone's coming!" said Rachel.

At that moment, the plump goblin lost his balance and both goblins tumbled right down the stairs.

The door opened and a blonde woman peered out. Behind her, the girls could see a room full of flustered film-makers. Two actors with red faces were scratching their heads, while the crew examined their cameras.

"I can't understand it," one of them was saying to himself. "I can't find anything wrong with it – but it just won't work!"

"I just can't seem to remember my lines," muttered one of the actors.

The blonde woman shook her head.

"What strange noises these old houses make," she said, closing the door again.

Rachel let out a sigh of relief.

"That was close!" said Kirsty.

"Come on!" Keira exclaimed, zooming down the stairs after the goblins. "We have to stop them causing any more trouble!"

Downstairs, the director and his crew were back on set, still trying to make the cameras work. The girls flew into the room and hovered close to the ceiling, trying to spot the goblins.

It was hard to see anything among the runners, extras and actors. But then Kirsty spotted one of Julianna's large frilly parasols. It was moving behind a red velvet sofa in the corner of the room. Four green feet were poking out from underneath it.

"There!" she cried, pointing.

As they flew lower, they saw that the goblins were still fighting over the enchanted clapperboard. Just then, the skinny goblin used it to tweak the plump goblin's nose. He gave a groan of pain.

"Listen to those creaks," said a runner as he trailed a cable along the edge of the room. "Anyone would think this place was haunted."

"They'll break it!" said Keira in an alarmed voice. "We have to stop them!"

Movie
Mischief

"But we can't do anything with the film crew in the room," said Rachel. "We'll be spotted."

Keira peeped down at the film crew. Actors, runners and camera operators were calling out to each other and rushing backwards and forwards, trying to understand what had gone wrong.

155

A sound technician had wedged her microphone in the old ceiling beams and three runners were trying to pull it free. The wardrobe lady was in a panic because half her costumes had gone missing, and the make-up artist's brushes had fallen through the cracks between the floorboards. The poor director was sitting in the middle of it all with his head in his hands.

"This is the last day of filming on location," he groaned. "Mrs Croft is coming back tomorrow. We have to get the wedding scene on tape by tonight."

The three friends stared at each other in alarm. They were running out of time!

"We can't stay here or we'll be spotted," said Kirsty. "Let's hide on the mantelpiece."

"Good idea," said Keira. "We can watch the goblins from there and wait for a chance to get the enchanted clapperboard back."

They fluttered over to the fireplace.
They had just darted behind a pretty
porcelain lady when the director jumped
to his feet.

"Quiet!" he boomed.

That made even the goblins stop
fighting and stick their heads out from
behind the parasol.

"I cannot create movie magic in these conditions," the director went on. "Get everyone in here! Let's set up a screen and watch the rushes until the equipment can be fixed."

"What are rushes?" asked Rachel as the director's team sprang into action.

"They're the scenes that were filmed the day before," Keira explained. "The director always checks them to make sure nothing went wrong and needs to be re-shot."

The girls watched as two runners pointed a projector at the white wall above Mrs Croft's sideboard. A production assistant carefully lifted a large reel of film out of a black leather case.

The room was soon packed full of actors, runners, camera operators and assistants.

"Let's make it dark in here," said the director.

A runner with a clipboard pulled the curtains shut and turned off the lights.

Then the production assistant pressed
'play', and the scenes that had been
filmed the day before were projected
onto Mrs Croft's white wall.

The room was dark and shadowy, but
in the light from the rushes, Kirsty saw
something moving behind the sofa.

"I think the goblins are trying to see
what's going on," she whispered.

"Let's get closer,"
Rachel suggested.

Under cover of
darkness, the
girls swooped
quickly down
from the
mantelpiece
and fluttered
closer to the goblins.

The goblins were watching the film scenes and scowling.

"Look at that soppy fairy rubbish!" said the plump one, folding his arms. "Who wants to watch films about pesky fairies, anyway?"

"Jack Frost would make a much better film," the skinny goblin agreed, tucking the enchanted clapperboard under his arm. "And I would be the star!"

"No, *I* would be the star!" insisted the plump goblin.

"No, me!"

162

"*Me!*"

"*Me!*"

The skinny goblin jumped up on top of the sideboard, standing right in front of the projector screen. Everyone in the room gasped – it looked as if he had appeared in the middle of the film scene!

"See how wonderful I look on screen?" he demanded.

He struck a pose and put his hand on his hip...and the enchanted clapperboard fell to the floor. The plump goblin made a dive for it.

"Quick – grab it!" cried Keira.

Fairy Film Stars

Kirsty, Rachel and Keira reached the enchanted clapperboard a second too late. The plump goblin was clutching it tightly to his chest.

"Give that back to Keira," said Rachel. "It doesn't belong to you."

"You're not having it, so there!" the goblin squeaked.

The director was frowning at the skinny goblin who had appeared in the middle of his scene.

"I certainly don't remember filming this," he said.

"Yes, and who's that ugly extra?" said Chad Stenning.

"Who are you calling ugly?" squawked the goblin, blowing a noisy raspberry at the star. "I'm the best-looking goblin in the whole world!"

"Oh no you're not!" snapped the plump goblin, jumping up beside him.

"Who hired these naughty extras?" demanded the director. "And where did they get those hideous costumes?"

"They think that the goblins are actors!" gasped Rachel.

The plump goblin gave the skinny one a hard shove. The outlines of their bodies filled the white wall behind them.

"I was born to be a star!" the skinny goblin yelled.

"No you weren't, I was!" the plump goblin squawked.

He flung the enchanted clapperboard down on the carpet in a temper.

"Someone get those extras out of here!" roared the director.

"This is our chance!" said Rachel.

As a runner jumped up to remove the goblins from the room, the three friends zipped towards the enchanted clapperboard. The film crew were staring at the goblins, so no one saw the little fairy land beside the enchanted clapperboard and shrink it down to fairy-size.

"I've got it!" she cried, lifting it up and hugging it tightly to her chest.

168

The runner was now chasing the goblins around the room, and everyone was shouting and pointing.

"Come on," cried Kirsty, shouting over the din. "Let's fly out to the garden before the goblins realise that the enchanted clapperboard has gone!"

They fluttered towards a gap in Mrs Croft's curtains and swooped out through the open window. The afternoon sunbeams were dazzling compared to the dark cottage.

"We did it!" declared Keira.

The three friends shared a joyful hug.
Just then, they heard Mrs Croft's front
door open. The goblins stomped out of
the cottage, scowling.

"I've had enough of learning about
making films!" the girls heard the plump
goblin complain. "And I'm going to tell
Jack Frost so!"

The goblins disappeared into the
woods, and Keira smiled at Rachel
and Kirsty.

"Thank you for all your help today," she said. "Now filming can get back to normal. It's time for your scene!"

With a graceful swish of her magic wand, she returned Kirsty and Rachel to their normal size. Kirsty straightened her handmaiden's tiara, ready to go inside.

"Our big moment has arrived at last!" smiled Rachel.

"I'm going to take the enchanted clapperboard back to Fairyland," explained Keira.

"But I've got a feeling that *The Starlight Chronicles* is going to be a sparkling success. Break a leg!"

"Break a leg!" called Kirsty and Rachel, waving happily.

Keira twirled her wand in a tiny circle. Then she disappeared in a burst of golden light, leaving behind a fizzing shower of stars.

A runner popped his head out of Mrs Croft's cottage.

"Are you coming in, girls?" he called. "The cameras are working again and we're ready for you."

Kirsty and Rachel hurried inside, their hearts fluttering with excitement. They arrived just in time to hear the director say some truly magical words.

"Lights! Camera! Action!"

Now Kirsty and Rachel
must help...

Jessie the Lyrics Fairy

Read on for a sneak peek...

"Rainspell Island, here we come!"
cheered Kirsty Tate, pointing ahead to
the green island which had just appeared
in view. She and her best friend Rachel
Walker were on the deck of a ferry,
heading off to the island, which was
a very special place. Not only was it
where the girls had first met, it was also
the place they'd had their very first fairy
adventure together.

"Nearly there," said Rachel. "I can't
wait to see The Angels again..."

Read Jessie the Lyrics Fairy to find out what
adventures are in store for Kirsty and Rachel!

Competition!

Keira the Film Star Fairy has created this special word wand just for you! Read the clues and write the answers in the boxes. The last letter of each word is the start of the next one. When you have all three answers, go online to enter.

1. **Where would you go to watch a film on a really big screen?**

2. **Can you complete this phrase: "Lights, camera, ___"?**

3. **Can you complete the name of this film about a fish: "Finding ___"?**

We will put all of the correct entries into a draw and select one winner to receive a special goody bag. You'll also star in a new Rainbow Magic story!

Enter online now at www.rainbowmagicbooks.co.uk

No purchase required. Only one entry per child.
Two prize draws will take place on 31 March 2012 and 30 June 2012.
Alternatively readers can send the three answers on a postcard to:
Rainbow Magic Keira the Film Star Fairy Competition,
Orchard Books, 338 Euston Road, London, NW1 3BH. Australian readers can write to: Rainbow Magic Keira the Film Star Fairy Competition, Hachette Children's Books, level 17/207 Kent St, Sydney, NSW 2000.
E-mail: childrens.books@hachette.com.au. New Zealand readers should write to Rainbow Magic Keira the Film Star Fairy Competition, 4 Whetu Place, Mairangi Bay, Auckland, NZ

Meet the
Pop Star Fairies

Kirsty and Rachel have to save Rainspell Island Music Festival after Jack Frost steals the Pop Star Fairies' musical clef necklaces!

www.rainbowmagicbooks.co.uk